Willie lived with his grandma in a tiny one-room apartment on the North Side of Chicago. It was 1942 and nothing came easy, not even a boy's dreams. Everything Willie loved best was there in that little apartment: Grandma, their radio, and the wad of tape and string Willie used as a baseball when he played stickball in the street.

It was Willie's grandma who taught him to love baseball. As they settled into their seats in front of the old radio, Willie would close his eyes and feel just like he was at Wrigley Field, his heart pumping to the sound of balls slamming into mitts, sending puffs of old leather dust into the afternoon sunlight as waves of fresh-cut grass tickled his nose. Someday, he knew, he would stand at home plate smashing a fastball deep into center field for a home run!

Willie pretended he was playing baseball no matter what he was doing. A trip to the store quickly became a series of stolen bases from the curb to the lamppost to the fire hydrant to the mailbox until he slid—SAFE!—at home, without breaking an egg!

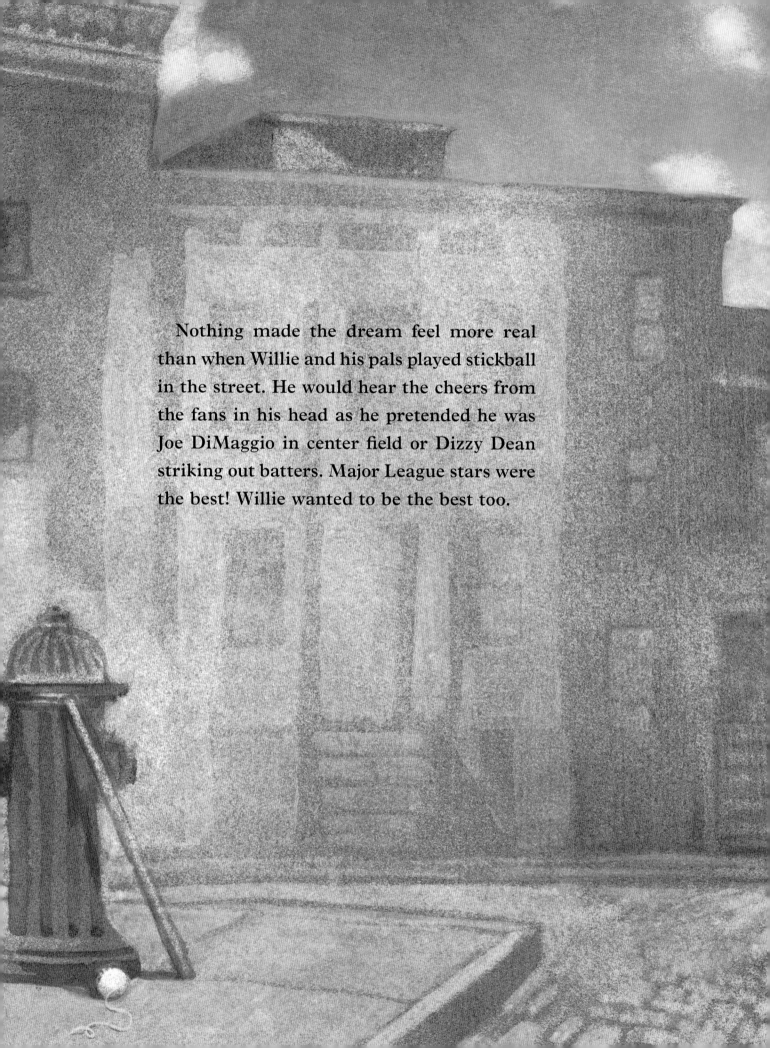

Nothing made the dream feel more real than when Willie and his pals played stickball in the street. He would hear the cheers from the fans in his head as he pretended he was Joe DiMaggio in center field or Dizzy Dean striking out batters. Major League stars were the best! Willie wanted to be the best too.

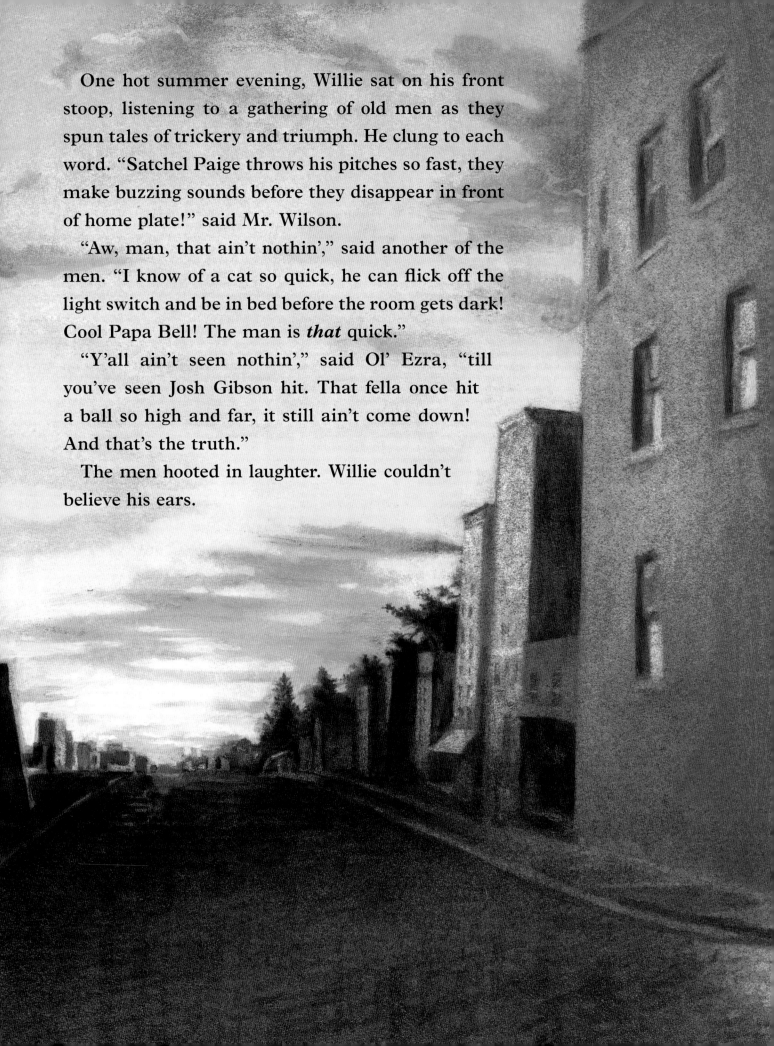

One hot summer evening, Willie sat on his front stoop, listening to a gathering of old men as they spun tales of trickery and triumph. He clung to each word. "Satchel Paige throws his pitches so fast, they make buzzing sounds before they disappear in front of home plate!" said Mr. Wilson.

"Aw, man, that ain't nothin'," said another of the men. "I know of a cat so quick, he can flick off the light switch and be in bed before the room gets dark! Cool Papa Bell! The man is *that* quick."

"Y'all ain't seen nothin'," said Ol' Ezra, "till you've seen Josh Gibson hit. That fella once hit a ball so high and far, it still ain't come down! And that's the truth."

The men hooted in laughter. Willie couldn't believe his ears.

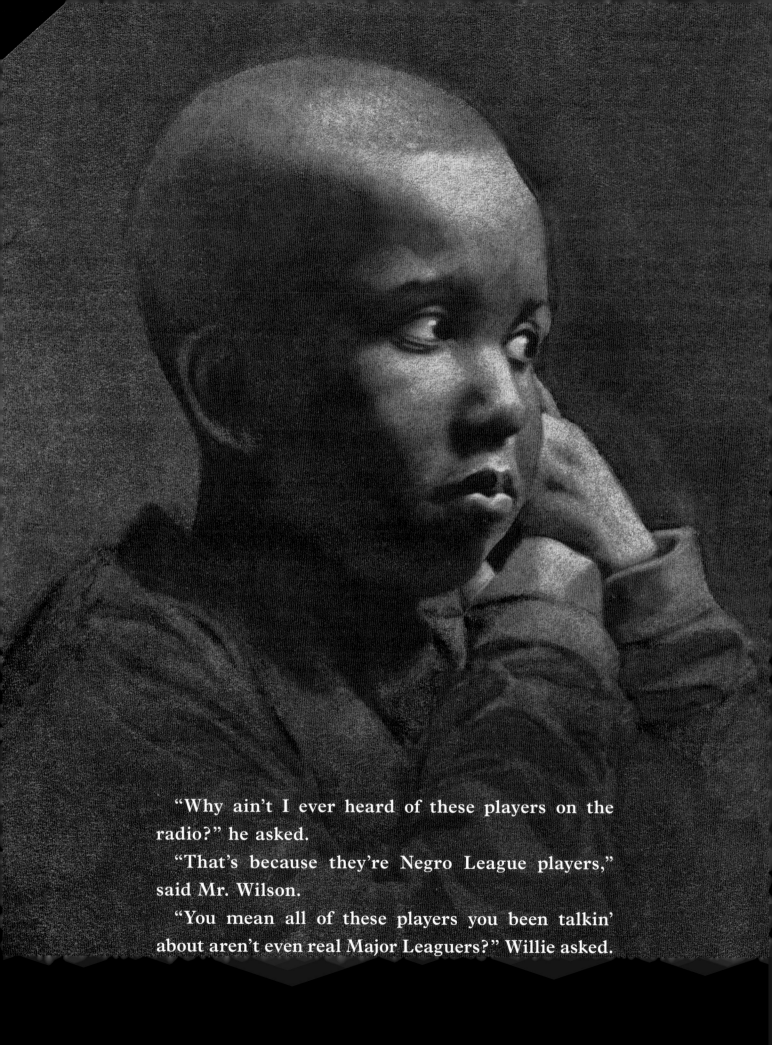

"Why ain't I ever heard of these players on the radio?" he asked.

"That's because they're Negro League players," said Mr. Wilson.

"You mean all of these players you been talkin' about aren't even real Major Leaguers?" Willie asked.

Ol' Ezra rose up from the steps and looked Willie right in the eyes. "Son," he said, "being a Major League ballplayer is about a lot more than how good a fella is. It's also about the color of his skin. And yours is the wrong color."

All of a sudden Willie felt all closed up inside. Almost like he was trapped in a box.

Of course, Willie wasn't the only boy with baseball dreams. He and his good pal Sean O'Carroll had spent hour after hour talking about how they were going to make it to the Major Leagues someday.

"I'm gonna smack balls over the outfield wall, just like the Babe!" Sean would say. "You and me, Willie. We'll work hard together and play on the same team."

Willie would usually laugh, but today he just dropped his head. He thought about how he and Sean couldn't sit together on the trolley. How they had to drink from separate water fountains at the park.

"Ol' Ezra tells me I ain't never gonna play in the Majors," said Willie.

Sean put his hand on Willie's shoulder.

"You don't know that for sure," he said. "Ol' Ezra may know a lot, but he doesn't know everything."

The next day they saw Ol' Ezra standing out on the stoop, talking with some men. One of them put something into Ezra's pocket and gave him a great big hug before driving away in a fancy-looking car. As the boys walked past, Ol' Ezra stopped Willie.

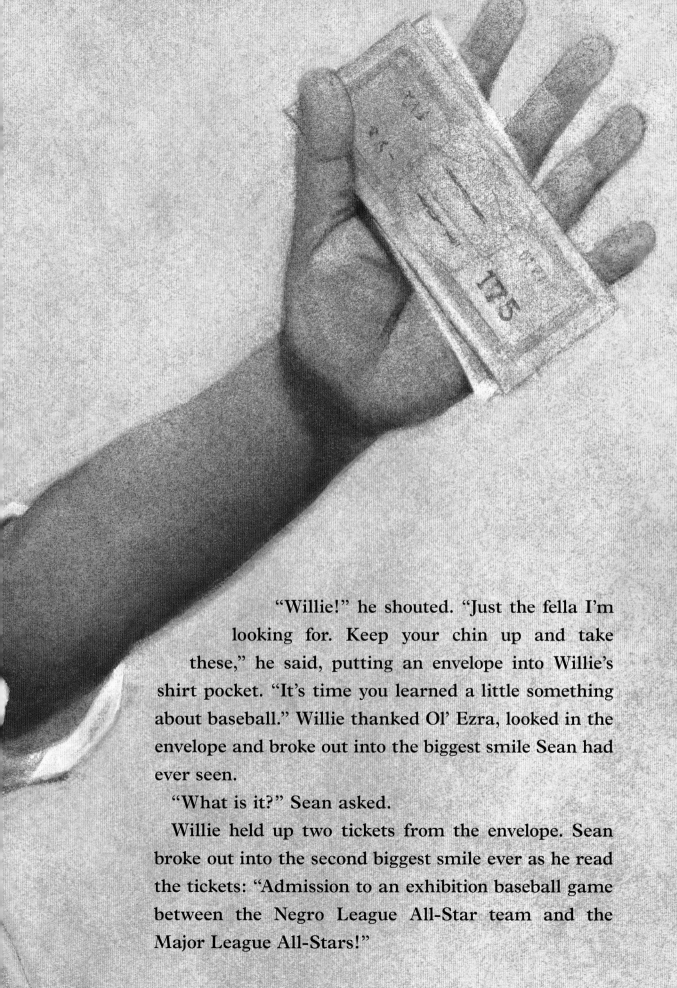

"Willie!" he shouted. "Just the fella I'm looking for. Keep your chin up and take these," he said, putting an envelope into Willie's shirt pocket. "It's time you learned a little something about baseball." Willie thanked Ol' Ezra, looked in the envelope and broke out into the biggest smile Sean had ever seen.

"What is it?" Sean asked.

Willie held up two tickets from the envelope. Sean broke out into the second biggest smile ever as he read the tickets: "Admission to an exhibition baseball game between the Negro League All-Star team and the Major League All-Stars!"

Willie couldn't believe his eyes. Here he was, in a place he never thought he would see. A place where men became legends. A place Willie and kids like him could only go in their imaginations. This was WRIGLEY FIELD!

Willie took it all in. He wanted to remember for Grandma every single detail. He would tell her how he and Sean saw all the greats, the very ones they heard play on the radio.

And then there were the Negro League players. A ragtag collection they were, in uniforms tattered and faded from too many trips up and down backcountry roads. Shoes softened and worn with age and memories of two or three games a day. Baseball gloves patched up, tied and retied too many times. These players joked around and played games in front of the dugout as they warmed up. *Don't they realize who it is they are going to play?* Willie wondered.

There was Satchel Paige, driving a
nail through a post with his infamous
"Bee Ball" pitch!

There was Josh Gibson just playing around, sending a ball so high into the sky, it probably wouldn't come down till midnight!

Willie and Sean saw through-the-leg catches and behind-the-back throws. The Negro Leaguers were fast and talented for sure, but could they really compete with the best?

The game was tough fought to the bitter end as each team played hard to win. But from the first pitch, the Negro League team seemed a bit hungrier for the victory. They stretched singles into doubles, doubles into triples and even stole home for a score! They hit harder, ran faster and just plain outmuscled the Major League team for the win.

The crowd went wild at the display they'd just seen,
and the Negro League players hugged each other in joy.

Then something happened that made Willie catch his breath. Two opposing players, one from each team, found their way through the hoopla and fray and met each other face-to-face atop the pitcher's mound. The whooping and hollering stopped with a jolt as the crowd watched in astonishment. Two players, one black, one white, shook hands—a nod of acknowledgment, if not acceptance, from White to Black.

AUTHOR'S NOTE

Back when baseball was first played, when it held promise for any dreamer with enough talent and luck, any man could put his skills on the line and go as far as his play would take him. It didn't matter if he was Black, Brown, or White. Baseball was, in a sense, young and open to all.

In 1888 all that changed when baseball, perhaps reflecting the social climate of the times, banned players of color from Major League participation. Untold dreams were snuffed out and superb talent was stifled.

Negro League Baseball was formed as an answer to the closed hand of Major League Baseball. It started out with ragtag teams called "Barnstormers." The teams were made up of talented players pulled together from wherever, who would travel the back roads in search of nothing more than a field to play on and a team to challenge. Free from the confines and rules of the Majors, the Negro League game evolved into a looser, faster, some would say more entertaining brand of baseball as promoters sought to increase fan attendance and keep the seats filled.

The Barnstormers had it rough. They traveled the dusty back roads of America, oftentimes playing several games in a single day for very meager pay. Along the way, they brought baseball to thousands of game-starved fans who would otherwise be denied the experience of this home-bred sport.

As the legend of the Negro League's best grew, it attracted the attention of Major League owners, who were fighting dwindling attendance as America fought in a war overseas. This led to opportunity: the All-Star games pitting Negro Leaguers versus Major Leaguers. Many such contests were held, and more often than not, the Negro Leaguers came out on top. Who knows how many dreams were kindled by their determination?

Willie and the All-Stars is about one such dream that may have been inspired by this period in the history of America's pastime.